For Sue Lin

This paperback version first published in Great Britain in 2011 by
Pavilion Children's Books
An imprint of Anova Books Ltd
10 Southcombe Street, London, W14 0RA

Text and illustration copyright © Nick Ward

The moral right of the author has been asserted

A CIP catalogue record for this book is available
from the British Library.

ISBN 978-1-84365-191-8

Printed in Italy

10 9 8 7 6 5 4 3 2 1

This book can be ordered direct from the publisher at the website: www.anovabooks.com

I Wish...

NICK WARD

PAVILION
CHILDREN'S

"I wish," said the little boy
with eyes shut tight,
"I wish I may,
I wish I might..."

Now that it's night time,
my teddy and I,
could open the window
and through it we'd fly...

Up to the moon,
to slide down its back,
scatter the stars through
the sky, inky black.

Make them crackle,
then fade and sparkle again,
as we fall through a cloud
and turn on the rain.

In a cloudburst shower,
Teddy and I
would splash into the sea,
as we dropped from the sky.

Sink under the waves,
leave a silvery trail,
to be lifted at once on
the hump of a whale.

Past galleons laden with
gold we would glide,
as a thousand bright fishes
flashed by our side.

And from a moonlit crag,
narrow and tall,
a lonely mermaid princess
would call.

Our whale would surge through the bubbling foam and sing us his song as we headed for home.

Then as the whale sailed
close to the shore,
Teddy and I would take
flight once more...

Over the rooftops,
through silent streets,
tap on the windows of
the world as it sleeps.

And as the town clock
started to chime,
we would fly on
towards morning time.

As a new morning sun
rose in the sky,
safely in bed with
Teddy I'd lie.

"I wish," said the little boy
with eyes burning bright,
"I wish I may,
I wish I might..."